UPTOWN

Bryan Collier

Henry Holt and Company

New York

Henry Holt and Company, LLC, *Publishers since 1866*

115 West 18th Street, New York, New York 10011

Henry Holt is a registered trademark of Henry Holt and Company, LLC

Published in Canada by Fitzhenry & Whiteside Ltd.,

195 Allstate Parkway, Markham, Ontario L3R 4T8.

Library of Congress Cataloging-in-Publication Data

Collier, Bryan.

Uptown / Bryan Collier.

Summary: A tour of the sights of Harlem, including the Metro-North train, brownstones, shopping on
125th Street, a barbershop, summer basketball, the Harlem Boys Choir, and sunset over the Hudson River.

[1. Harlem (New York, N.Y.)—Fiction. 2. Afro-Americans—Fiction.] I. Title.

PZ7.C67759Up 2000 [E]—dc21 99-31774

ISBN 0-8050-5721-8 / First Edition—2000

The artist used watercolor and collage to create the illustrations for this book.

Designed by Martha Rago

Printed in the United States of America on acid-free paper. ∞

3   5   7   9   10   8   6   4   2

Dedicated to the loving memory of
my mother, Esther Collier.
To God be the Glory.

Uptown is a caterpillar.

Well, it's really the Metro-North train as it eases over the Harlem River.

Uptown is chicken and waffles served around the clock.

At first it seems like a weird combination, but it works.

Uptown is a row of brownstones.

I like the way they come together
when you look at them down the block.
They look like they're made of chocolate.

Uptown
is
weekend **shopping**
on
125th Street.

The vibe is always jumping
as people bounce to their own
rhythms.

Uptown is a stage.

The Apollo Theater
has showcased the greatest
entertainers in the world.

I hope we can get good seats.

My grandfather says, "Jazz and Harlem are a perfect match—just like chicken and waffles."

Uptown is a barbershop.

It's a place where last night's ball game can be more important than what style haircut you want.

Uptown

is a

Van Der Zee

photograph.

I saw a picture from before my dad was even born—a picture of my grandparents' wedding day!

Uptown is summer basketball at the Ruckers.

Anyone can rise up
and be a superstar for a day.

Uptown is canvas awnings on the windows to block the sun.

It's like the buildings are all dressed up.

Uptown is little sisters.

They're on their way to church in matching yellow dresses.

Uptown
is the
orange sunset
over the
Hudson River.

That means it's time for the streetlights
to come on and for me to get home
and get changed.

Uptown is
a **song** sung
by the Boys Choir
of Harlem.

Each

note

floats through the air

and lands

like a butterfly.

Harlem world, my world.

Uptown is home.

Uptown
B C